DISNEY
◆ PRINCESS

MULAN

A Story of Courage

Adapted by Amy Adair
Illustrated by the Disney Storybook Artists

Published by Louis Weber, C.E.O., Publications International, Ltd.
7373 North Cicero Avenue, Lincolnwood, Illinois 60712

Ground Floor, 59 Gloucester Place, London W1U 8JJ

Customer Service: 1-800-595-8484 or customer_service@pilbooks.com

www.pilbooks.com

p i kids is a registered trademark of Publications International, Ltd.

Manufactured in China.

8 7 6 5 4 3 2 1

ISBN-13: 978-1-4127-6778-1

ISBN-10: 1-4127-6778-4

pi kids ® publications international, ltd.

Long ago a girl named Mulan lived in a small village in China. She was very beautiful. But she was also very smart and brave. Mulan's family wanted nothing more than for Mulan to find a husband to uphold the family honor. Today was the day that she was going to meet the Matchmaker.

Mulan wanted to make a good impression, so she practiced reciting some of the qualities that made a good wife. "Quiet, graceful, and punctual," she said.

Mulan nervously played with her hair, which was tied up in a ribbon. She dressed in a beautiful gown that her mother had given her. And Grandmother Fa had given her Cri-Kee, a cricket, for good luck.

Mulan was surprised when she looked up and saw her own reflection. She was as pretty as a porcelain doll, but she did not feel like herself.

Unfortunately, the important meeting with the Matchmaker did not go very well.

"Fa Mulan," the Matchmaker called.

"Present," Mulan said, raising her hand.

"Speaking without permission," the Matchmaker scolded. "Now pour the tea," she ordered Mulan.

And that is when things got worse for Mulan. First, she got ink on the Matchmaker's face. Then she spilled hot tea on the Matchmaker. After that, the Matchmaker's dress caught on fire!

"You are a disgrace!" the Matchmaker screamed. "You may look like a bride, but you will never be one. And you will certainly never *ever* bring honor to your family!"

Ashamed, Mulan ran home.

Far away in the Imperial City, the Emperor was hearing bad news, too. The Huns were attacking China. "Send out notices to all my people," said the Emperor. "We need one man from every family to help defend our country."

Chi Fu, the Emperor's adviser, delivered the news to the Fa family.

Mulan did not have a brother, so her father had to serve. But her father could barely walk without using his crutch. Mulan knew he could never fight in a battle.

"Father, you can't go!" Mulan yelled.

"Silence!" Chi Fu shouted. "You should teach your daughter to be silent in a man's presence."

"Mulan, don't dishonor me," her father said.

Later that night, Mulan realized what she had to do. Her father was too ill to fight, but he was too proud to defy orders.

"I can't let him go," Mulan said to herself.

Mulan took out her father's sword. She decided that she would disguise herself as a man and take his place.

Late that night, she cut off her long, beautiful black hair. She put on her father's heavy armor. Then she stole her father's horse Khan from the stable and rode into the stormy night.

The next morning, when the Fa family discovered that Mulan had left to join the army, they were very sad. They knew that if Mulan were caught disguised as a man, she would be killed!

The next day, Mulan rode into the army camp. She presented her father's papers to Captain Li Shang, the general's son.

"My name is Ping," said Mulan, trying to make her voice sound like a man's. She had to fool everyone into thinking she was a man, because women were not allowed to fight.

At first Mulan didn't do very well as the Emperor's army trained for battle, but she kept trying. Soon she became a good soldier. In fact, Mulan helped win a battle against the Huns. But she was badly wounded in the process.

When the doctor examined Mulan, he discovered her secret. The captain and the rest of the army were stunned. They left Mulan behind.

"I should have never left home," Mulan sighed.

Suddenly Mulan heard something strange. She looked down the mountain. Shan-Yu, the leader of the Huns, was still alive! "I have to do something," Mulan said. She raced to the Imperial City.

Everyone in the city was celebrating Captain Li Shang's victory. "Li Shang!" Mulan yelled. "The Huns are in the Imperial City!"

"Go home!" Li Shang ordered Mulan.

Mulan tried to warn the Emperor's guards, but they wouldn't listen to her, either. The Huns captured the Emperor.

Mulan had an idea. She dressed her three soldier friends like women to distract Shan-Yu's men. Then she rescued the Emperor!

Afterward the Emperor confronted Mulan at the palace, in front of thousands of people. He bowed before her. Everyone else bowed down, too.

Mulan rushed home to her family and knelt down before her father in the garden.

"Beloved father, I only wanted to help you," said Mulan. "I didn't mean to dishonor our family."

"Having such a brave daughter," said Mulan's father, "is the greatest honor of all!"

Mulan: A Story of Courage

Courage means that no matter how frightened you may be or how big the challenge is ahead of you, you make up your mind to do your very best. Courage takes strength.

Sometimes that strength is physical, like using your muscles. But often it's more important to have a different kind of strength, the kind of strength that comes from believing in what you are doing.

Mulan wasn't born to be a soldier, but she believed that she could help her family and her country by being courageous and working hard. And that is exactly what she did!